Ready Set Go Books, an Open Hearts Big Dreams Project

Special thanks to Ethiopia Reads donors and staff for believing in this project and helping get it started-- and for arranging printing, distribution, and training in Ethiopia.

Copyright © 2020 Ready Set Go Books

ISBN: 979-8617101555
Library of Congress Control Number: 2020925014

Republished: 12/23/20

Thank you to the generous team who gave their time and talents to make this book possible.

Creative Directors
Caroline Kurtz
Jane Kurtz
Kenny Rasmussen

Translator
Bezabeh Belachew

TROUBLE
ተክሌ

WRITTEN BY JANE KURTZ

ILLUSTRATED BY DURGA YAEL BERNHARD

Trouble always found Tekleh. He didn't mean to get stung by poking a stick into a line of marching ants. He didn't mean to make dust fly onto the roasting coffee beans.

ተክሌ ሁሌ ችግር ውስጥ እንደገባ ነው፡፡ ያኔ በሰልፍ የሚንዙትን ጉንዳኖች በእንጨት ሲነካካ ይነክሱኛል ብሎ አላሰበም ነበር፡፡ አንዴም ሲጫወት ያቦነነው አቧራ የሚቆላው ቡና ውስጥ ይገባል ብሎ ፈጽሞ አልጠበቀም፡፡

And when he watched the family goats, he always meant to tend them carefully.

የቤተሰቡንም ፍየሎች ጠብቅ ሲባል፣ እነሱን በደንብ መንከባከብ ፍላጎቱ ነበር።

Finally, one day, Tekleh's father took a piece of wood and carved a gebeta board. "Now," he said, "we will have no more problems. A gebeta game always keeps a young boy out of trouble."

አንድ ቀን የተከሌ አባት እንጨት ጠርቦ የገበጣ መጫወቻ ሰራ። አባቱም ‹ከእንግዲህ ወዲህ ችግሮች አያጋጥሙንም። የገበጣ ጨዋታ ልጆች ችግር ውስጥ እንዳይገቡ ይጠብቃል።› ብሎ ተናገረ።

The next morning, Tekleh meant to head straight to the goats' grazing place in the hills. But, far in the distance, something was happening on the path.

በማግሥቱ ጠዋት ተክሌ ፍየሎቹን ወደሚያሰማራበት የግጦሽ ኮረብታ ለመሄድ አሰበ ነበር። ነገር ግን መንገዱን ሲጀምር ከሩቁ አንድ ነገር አየ።

Ah-hah. It was a group of traders with their dusty, musky camels. "Is there no wood in this country?" one of them asked. "We found only a few sticks for our fire."

"Of course there is wood," Tekleh said. He held up his gebeta board.

"Thank you," the man said. He grabbed the board and threw it on the fire.

ለካስ ከአቢራማ ግመሎቻቸው ጋር የሚዳዙ ነጋዴዎች ነበሩ። ከነጋዴዎቹም
አንዱ ‹እዚህ አገር እንጨትም የለ እንዴ? ለእሳት ማንደጃ ያገኘነው ጭራሮ
ብቻ ነው።› ብሎ ተናገረ።

‹እንጨትማ በደንብ አለ› በማለት ተክሌ የገበጣ መጫወቻውን ከፍ
አድርጎ አሳየው። ነጋዴውም ‹አመሰግናለሁ› ብሎ የተክሌን ገበጣ መጫወቻ
እሳት ውስጥ ወረወረው።

Tekleh set up such a howling that the traders' ears hurt. "Take this fine knife," one cried, "and stop that noise."

Tekleh was sad, but what could be done now? Down the path he went with his two goats and the fine knife.

ተክሌ የገበጣ መጫወቻው ሲቃጠል ነጋዴዎቹ ጆሯቸውን እስከሚያማቸው ድረስ በሃዘን ጩኸቱን ለቀቀ። አንዱም ነጋዴ ጮክ ብሎ ‹ጩኸትክን አቁምና ይህንን ጥሩ ቢላ ውሰድ› አለው።

ተክሌ በጣም አዝኖ ነበር። ግን አሁን ምን ማድረግ ይቻላል? ሁለቱ ፍየሎቹንና አዲሱ ቢላውን ይዞ መንገዱን ቀጠለ።

Before long, he saw a man sitting in the long grass. "Here," the man said. "A knife is not a thing for a young boy. Why don't you let me have it to skin the little dik-dik that will soon be caught in my trap?"

ተክሌ ብዙም ሳይቆይ አንድ ሰው ረጅም ሳር አጠገብ ተቀምጦ አየ። ሰውየውም ሕማ ለትንሽ ልጅ ቢላ ጥሩ አይደለም። ለምን በወጥመድ የምይዛትን የሚዳቋ ቆዳ እንድገፍበት ለኔ አትሰጠኝም፣ ብሎ ጠየቀው።

Tekleh was sorry to think of such a shy and delicate animal becoming a meal. But people must eat. So he said, "What will you give me if I give you this fine knife?"

The man held out his masinko. "My family needs food even more than music."

ሚዳቋን የመሰለች ትንሽና ሰላማዊ እንስሳ ለሰው ምግብ እንደምትሆን ሲያስብ ተክሌ በጣም አዘነ። ነገር ግን ሰዎች መብላት አለባቸው። ስለዚህም ተክሌ ሰውየውን ‹ይህን ጥሩ ቢላ ብሰጥህ እንተስ ምን ትሰጠኛለህ?› አለው። ሰውየውም ማሲንቆውን አወጣና ‹ከሙዚቃ የበለጠ ቤተሰቤ የሚያስፈልገው ምግብ ነው› አለ።

So off Tekleh went with his two goats and his masinko, making a fine noise, until he came upon a group of musicians shaking their shoulders as they danced. "Why don't you give us that masinko to play at the wedding feast?" one said. "You take this drum instead."

ተክሌም ሁለቱን ፍየሎቹና ማሲንቆውን ይዞ ጉዞውን ቀጠለ። በማሲንቆውም ግሩም ዜማ እየተጫወተ ሲጓዝ እስክስታ የሚወርዱ ሰዎች መንገድ ላይ አገኘ። ከነሱም አንዱ ‹እስቲ ማሲንቆህን ስጠንና የሰርግ ድግስ ላይ እንጫወትበት። እንካ አንተ ይህን ከበሮ ውሰድ› አለው።

Why not? Tekleh tucked the drum under his arm and tagged after them to the wedding, where the red smell of spices filled the air.

ተክሌ ከበሮውን በጁ አቅፎ ሰዎቹን እየተከተለ ወደ ሠርጉ ሄደ። አየሩም በቅመማ ቅመም ሽታ ታውዶ ነበር።

In the swirl of music and dancing, no one noticed Tekleh sampling the wedding feast. When one of the cooks finally chased him away, Tekleh trotted off with his two goats and his drum.

ዘፈኑና ጭፈራው ደርቶ ስለነበር ተክሌ የድግሱን ምግብ ሲቀማምስ ማንም አላየውም፡፡ በመጨረሻም ከምግብ አዘጋጆቹ አንዱ ስታባረው ፍየሎቹንና ከበሮውን ይዞ መሮጥ ጀመረ፡፡

The path was hot, and Tekleh stopped to watch a lizard sunning itself on a rock. His mother had told him not to touch lizards, but this one was so mysterious and still— and it could eat flies and mosquitoes in the house. So he popped it into his bag.

ተክሌ በሚሞቀው መንገድ ሲጓዝ አንድ እንሽላሊት ፀሐይ
ሲሞቅ ለማየት ቆመ። እናቱ ከዚህ በፊት እንሽላሊት እንዳይነካ
አስጠንቅቃው ነበር። ነገር ግን ይህ እንሽላሊት ልዩ ይመስላል፤
ቤትም ውስጥ ዝንብና ትንኝ ሊበላ ይችላል። ስለዚህ ተክሌ
እንሽላሊቱን ቦርሳው ውስጥ ከተተው።

When he found a shady cornfield, Tekleh took out his drum and began to thump. Three monkeys leaped out of the corn and scampered off. The farmer ran over. "Stay here and make that wonderful noise all afternoon," he said, "and I will give you a bag full of corn."

ቀጥሎም ተክሌ የበቆሎ ማሳ ጥላ ውስጥ ገብቶ ከበሮውን
ይመታ ጀመር። የከበሮውን ድምፅ ሲሰሙ ሶስት ጦጣዎች
ከበቆሎው እርሻ ወጥተው ይሮጡ ጀመር። ባለ እርሻው ወደ
ተክሌ እየሮጠ ሄዶ ፡በል እዚህ ቁጭ በልና ያንን አስደሳች
የከበሮ ድምፅ ቀኑን ሙሉ ተጫወት። እኔም አንድ ስልቻ
በቆሎ እስጥሃለው።፡፡ አለው።

As early evening shadows crawled across the ground, Tekleh took his corn, traded the drum for a fat papaya, and set off for home. A woman called out to him. "Salaam. Where did you find that papaya? I would like to get one for my children who have been sick."

Tekleh looked at the children. "Here," he said. "Let me make you a gift of this corn and the papaya."

ፀሐይ መጥለቅ ስትጀምር፤ ቀኑም ጨለምለም ሲል ተክሌ በቆሎውንና ከበሮውን ይዞ ጉዞውን ቀጠለ። መንገድ ላይም ከበሮውን በፓፓያ ቀይሮ ወደ ቤቱ ማምራት ጀመረ። አንዲት ሴትዮ መንገድ ላይ አይታው፤ ‹ሰላም ፓፓያውን ከየት አገኘኸው?› ብላ ጠየቀችው። ‹ለታመሙት ልጆቼ እንዲህ አይነት ፓፓያ ባገኝ እንዴት ደስ ባለኝ።› አለችው።

ተክሌም ልጆቹን አየና ‹እንኩ በቆሎውንና ፓፓያውን ውሰዱ። የኔ ስጦታ ነው።› አላቸው።

"Come in," the woman said. She blew on the fire and stirred the lentils. While Tekleh scooped up the lentils with his injera, he watched the children playing their gebeta game. Then he coaxed the goats out of the neighbor's garden, said goodbye, and started down the path.

Suddenly, he heard footsteps. The littlest girl was running after him, holding out the gebeta board.

ሴትዮዋም ፥ና ወደ ቤት ግባ፥ ብላ ጠራችው። እሳቱን ኡፍ ብላ ምስር ወጥ ማማሰል ጀመረች። ተክሌም ምስሩን በእንጀራ እየበላ ልጆቹ ገበጣ ሲጫወቱ ይመለከት ጀመር። በልቶም ሲጨርስ ፍየሎቹን ከጎሮ ሰብስቦ ሰዎቹን ተሰናብቶ መንገዱን ቀጠለ።

ድንገት ከጀርባው የሰው እርምጃ ሰማ። ትንሿ ልጅ የገበጣ መጫወቻቸውን ልትሰጠው እየተከተለችው ነበር።

So it was that Tekleh came home with two goats, one lizard, and a gebeta board. His father patted him on the head with pride.

"How well fed and contented the goats are today," he said to his family. "Did I not tell you? A gebeta board never fails to keep a young boy out of trouble."

ተክሌ ሁለት ፍየሎች፥ አንድ እንሽላሊትና፥ አንድ የገበጣ መጫወቻ ይዞ ቤቱ ገባ። አባቱም በልጁ በጣም ኮርቶ ጭንቅላቱን ይደባብሰው ጀመር።

የተከሌ አባት ‹ዛሬ ፍየሎቹ በደንብ የጠገቡና የተደሰቱ ይመስላሉ› ብሎ ለቤተሰቡ
ተናገረ። ‹ነግሪያችሁ የለ? የገበጣ መጫወቻ ሁሌ ልጅ ችግር ውስጥ እንዳይገባ
ይጠብቃል› አላቸው።

GLOSSARY

dik-dik (dik-dik):
a very small antelope

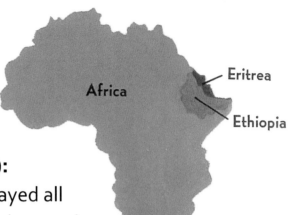

Africa

Eritrea

Ethiopia

gebeta (GUH-buh-tuh):
a popular board game played all
over the world, also called mancala

injera (in-JE-rah):
a large spongy pancake used as bread at most
meals in Eritrea and Ethiopia

mashella (mah-SHULL-ah):
sorghum, a grass grown for its grain

masinko (mah-SINK-oh):
a one-stringed fiddle with a diamond-shaped
sound box, a thick horsehair string, and a
curved wooden bow

Tekleh (TUK-kuh-luh):
literally translated as "to plant"

ABOUT THE LANGUAGE

Amharic is a Semetic language -- in fact, the world's second-most widely spoken Semetic language, after Arabic. Starting in the 12th century, it became the Ethiopian language that was used in official transactions and schools and became widely spoken all over Ethiopia.

Amharic is written with its own characters -- over **260** of them. Eritrea and Ethiopia share this alphabet, and they are the only countries in Africa to develop a writing system centuries ago that is still in use today!

ABOUT READY SET GO BOOKS

Reading has the power to change lives, but many children and adults in Ethiopia cannot read. One reason is that Ethiopia doesn't have enough books in local languages to give people a chance to practice reading. Ready Set Go books wants to close that gap and open a world of ideas and possibilities for kids and their communities.

When you buy a Ready Set Go book, you provide critical funding to create and distribute more books.

Learn more at: http://openheartsbigdreams.org/book-project/

Ready Set Go 10 Books

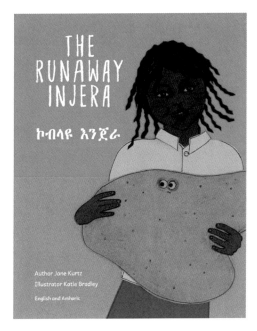

In **2018**, Ready Set Go Books decided to experiment by trying a few new books in larger sizes.

Sometimes it was the art that needed a little more room to really shine. Sometimes the story or non-fiction text was a bit more complicated than the short and simple text used in most of our current early reader books.

We called these our "Ready Set Go **10**" books as a way to show these ones are bigger and also sometimes have more words on the page. The response has

been great so now our Ready Set Go **10** books are a significant number of our titles. We are happy to hear feedback on these new books and on all our books.

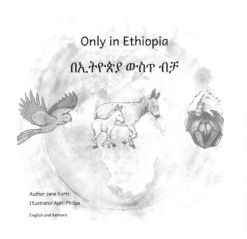

Only in Ethiopia

በኢትዮጵያ ውስጥ ብቻ

Author Jane Kurtz
Illustrator April Philips

English and Amharic

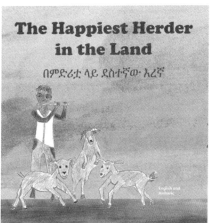

The Happiest Herder
in the Land

በምድሪቷ ላይ ደስተኛው እረኛ

English and Amharic

Where Do Dreams Grow?

ሕልሞች እውን የሚሆኑት የት ነው?

English and Amharic

Author Jane Kurtz
Illustrator Beth Molla

OPEN HEARTS BIG DREAMS

Led by Ellenore Angelidis in collaboration with author Jane Kurtz, Open Hearts Big Dreams began as a volunteer organization, with a mission to provide sustainable funding and strategic support to Ethiopia Reads. OHBD has now grown to be its own non-profit organization supporting literacy, art, and technology for young people in Ethiopia.

Ellenore Angelidis comes from a family of teachers who believe education is a human right, and opportunity should not depend on your birthplace. As the adoptive mother of a little girl who was born in Ethiopia and learned to read in the U.S., as well as an aspiring author, she finds the challenge of positively impacting literacy hugely compelling!

About Ethiopia Reads

Ethiopia Reads was started by volunteers in places like Grand Forks, North Dakota; Denver, Colorado; San Francisco, California; and Washington D.C. who wanted to give the gift of reading to more kids in Ethiopia.

One of the founders, Jane Kurtz, learned to read in Ethiopia where she spent most of her childhood and where the circle of life has come around to bring her Ethiopian-American grandchildren. As a children's book author, Jane is the driving force behind Open Hearts Big Dreams Ready Set Go Books - working to create the books that inspire those just learning to read.

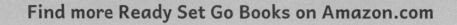

Find more Ready Set Go Books on Amazon.com

To view all available titles, search "Ready Set Go Ethiopia" or scan QR code

 Chaos

 Talk Talk Turtle

 The Glory of Gondar

 We Can Stop the Lion

 Not Ready!

 Fifty Lemons

 Count For Me

 Too Brave

 Tell Me What You Hear

Made in the USA
Las Vegas, NV
15 April 2024

88703136R00026